Fun

Harcourt, Inc.

Orlando   Austin   New York

San Diego   Toronto   London

Requests for permission to make copies of any part of the work should be submitted online
at www.harcourt.com/contact or mailed to the following address: Permissions Department,
Harcourt, Inc., 6277 Sea Harbor Drive, Orlando, Florida 32887-6777.

www.HarcourtBooks.com

Library of Congress Cataloging-in-Publication Data
Weeks, Sarah.
Bunny fun/Sarah Weeks; illustrated by Sam Williams.
    p.   cm.
Summary: A lively young rabbit finds many ways to have fun—and cause havoc—on a rainy day.
[1. Play—Fiction.   2. Rabbits—Fiction.   3. Stories in rhyme.]   I. Williams, Sam, 1955– ill.   II. Title.
PZ8.3.W4215Bun   2007
[E]—dc22   2006009246
ISBN 978-0-15-205838-8

First edition
    H G F E D C B A

Printed in Singapore

The illustrations in this book were done in charcoal, pastel, and watercolor on hot-press paper.
The display type was set in OptiBernhard Gothic. The text type was set in Sassoon Sans.
Color separations by Colourscan Co. Pte. Ltd., Singapore
Printed and bound by Tien Wah Press, Singapore
Production supervision by Pascha Gerlinger
Designed by April Ward

To Luis V.
—S. W.

For Mr. Sam—making life fun!
—S. W.

Drip-drop rainy day.
Bunny can't go out to play.

Waiting for the sunny sun,
time to have some...

Bunny fun!

Hip-hop!
Clip-clop!

in Mama's shoes.

Snip-snip!
Clippity-clip!

Bunny fun

with Papa's news.

Dribble, scribble.
Scribble, dribble.

Bunny fun

with drippy red.

Don't peek.
Hide-and-seek.
Bunny
underneath the bed.

Roll, pat,
Bunny fun.

Chitchat,

Bunny fun.

Vroom! Vroom!

Bunny fun.

Bunny fun inside a box.

Bunny fun

in slippery socks.

Busy building

Bunny Town.

Funny Bunny

upside down.

Ha-ha!
Bunny fun.

Cha-cha!

Bunny fun.

Look Bunny! Sunny day!
Rainy rain has gone away.

Uh-oh . . .
drippy swing.

Slippery drippy
everything.

No more **Bunny fun** today?

I see somewhere
we can play!

Hippity hippity hip hooray!